To Hazel and Easton,

Best wishes.

from,

Monica M. Graham

Johny
and the *Extraordinary* Caterpillar

STORY AND ILLUSTRATIONS BY

MONICA M. GRAHAM

Moonglade Press
Publishing New Works by Uncommon Voices
Distributed by IngramSpark

ISBN: 978-0-9987639-1-0

Library of Congress Control Number: 2018965359

Printed in the U.S.A.

Book design by Thomas Osborne

This book is dedicated to David, Rich and Si.

Johny is a shy cottontail bunny
with soft gray fur and long upright ears.
He lives in a pretty pasture near a pond.

There is a small house

with a big deck for him to burrow under.

Johny loves his home, but he is lonely.

He used to play with his brothers and sisters

until they all grew up and left home,

now he is all alone.

"I wish I could find a friend,"

thought Johny. He had seen a frog and a duck

near his house, but he was too shy to ask if they

would play with him.

One morning

Johny woke up and went to eat

his breakfast of yummy grass

like he always did.

That's when he was startled

by a striped worm with lots of little legs.

"Hi, I am Oscar the extraordinary caterpillar,

who are you?" the caterpillar asked.

"I'm Johny," the bunny replied.

"Extraordinary? Why do you say that?"

asked Johny shyly.

Before Oscar could explain

the sky grew dark,

and the wind blew in big gusts.

A bolt of lightning zigzagged

through the morning sky.

"It's going to rain, quick follow me,"

said Johny.

Johny ran under the deck,

Oscar followed as fast as he could.

"Welcome to my home," said Johny.

"Thank you. It is very cozy."

"We can stay here until the storm passes,"

said Johny.

"Now tell me, what makes you

so extraordinary?"

"You will see, but first gather

all of your friends together," replied Oscar.

"Well, I don't have any friends," Johny said sadly.

"I will help you make friends," Oscar replied.

"In the flower bed by the house lives a frog.

You can invite him.

Next, invite the quails who live in the bushes."

"I can do that," said Johny nervously.

"By the rock wall

at the corner of the lawn lives the lizard,

you can invite him too.

Then go down the hill to the pond

and invite the duck."

"I can do that," said Johny.

"Finally near the stump

of the fallen tree lives a rabbit,

you can invite her."

"I can do that and I will," Johny said bravely.

"Get everyone together tomorrow morning

and bring them to the lilac bush.

I'll be waiting for all of you," said Oscar.

Oscar and Johny played together

the rest of the afternoon and into the evening

until they were so tired they fell asleep.

Johny woke up early

the next morning.

He was too excited to eat breakfast,

he had a lot of friends to meet,

and tell about Oscar.

First, he went to the flower bed by the house

and told the frog about the special caterpillar.

Johny shyly asked the frog to help him invite

the other animals.

Together they hopped

over to the bushes where the quails lived

and asked the quails to come along.

Johny,

the frog, and the quails all went

to the rock wall and met the lizard.

The lizard joined them,

and they all went to the pond and told

the duck about the caterpillar too.

They waited until last

to tell the rabbit about Oscar.

The frog, the quails,

the duck, the lizard, and the rabbit

followed Johny to the lilac bush.

Oscar was waiting

for them just like he promised.

"Hello everyone," Oscar said.

"Today I am a caterpillar,

and in ten days I will be able to fly."

"No way," they shouted.

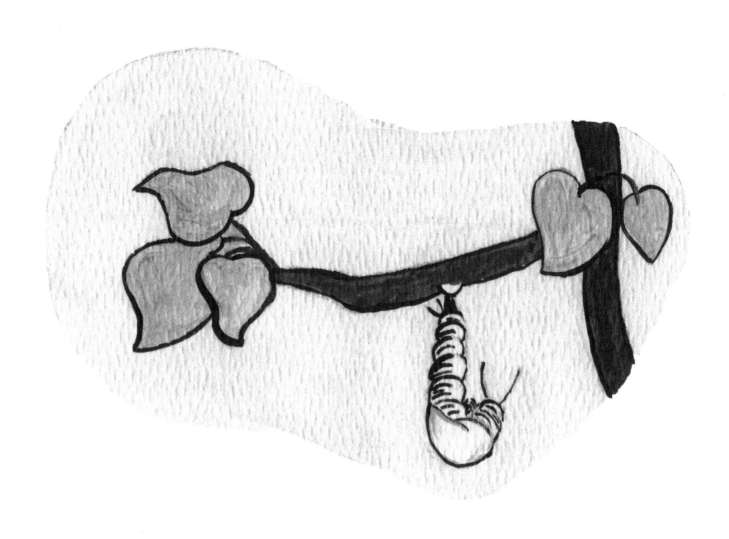

"Yes I will, you just watch.

I will cover myself in a casing

called a chrysalis, and then something

extraordinary will happen.

I want all of you to come back in ten days,

and you will see."

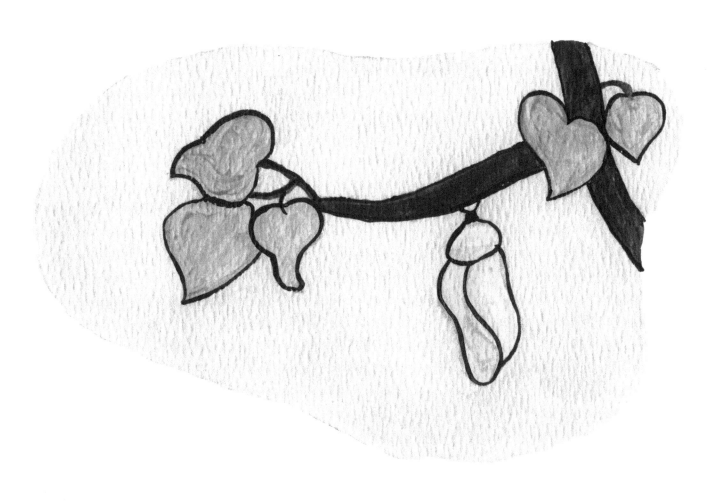

Oscar climbed high up

the lilac branch and fastened himself to it.

When he was done, he looked

like a very small leaf.

They all stared up at him curiously.

To pass the time,

they played together. They chased
each other around the lilac bush
and took turns looking up at the leaf.

On the tenth day, they looked up
and saw that the chrysalis was clear. They saw
a butterfly wing coming out of the opening.
Before long a whole butterfly came out
and rested on the lilac bush.

"What happened

to Oscar the caterpillar?"

asked the duck.

"It's me," the butterfly said.

"I am now a Monarch butterfly."

"Wow," the duck said.

"You are special," said Johny.

"It's amazing,"

said the frog.

He clapped, and so did everyone else.

"Thank you," said Oscar.

"But I didn't do this alone, nature helped.

It's called metamorphosis,

changing from

a caterpillar to a butterfly,

and it is extraordinary."

"Yes, it is," agreed Johny.

Oscar flew up and around everyone.

"I will migrate

in a few weeks, and fly South.

I can be your friend until then."

"You will always be our friend," Johny said.

"Even when you are not here.

You not only changed into a butterfly

but you brought us all together.

We are all friends now,

and that is

extraordinary."

CPSIA information can be obtained
at www.ICGtesting.com
Printed in the USA
BVHW021515040419
544551BV00002B/6/P

9 780998 763910